Picture This

ANTHONY HYDE

Picture This

Grass Roots Press

First published in 2011 by Grass Roots Press

The Good Reads series is funded in part by the Government of Canada's Office of Literacy and Essential Skills.

Grass Roots Press also gratefully acknowledges the financial support for its publishing programs provided by the following agencies: the Government of Canada through the Canada Book Fund and the Government of Alberta through the Alberta Foundation for the Arts.

Alberta Foundation for the Arts

Grass Roots Press would also like to thank ABC Life Literacy Canada for their support. Good Reads® is used under licence from ABC Life Literacy Canada.

Library and Archives Canada Cataloguing in Publication

Hyde, Anthony, 1946–
    Picture this / Anthony Hyde.

(Good reads series)
ISBN 978-1-926583-34-1

    1. Readers for new literates. I. Title. II. Series: Good reads series (Edmonton, Alta.)

PS8565.Y34P53 2011   428.6'2   C2011-902715-1

Printed and bound in Canada.

Distributed to libraries and educational and community organizations by
Grass Roots Press
www.grassrootsbooks.net

Distributed to retail outlets by
HarperCollins Canada Ltd.
www.harpercollins.ca

To Miss Lynn, Miss Earl, Miss Smith,
Miss Mackenzie, and Miss Hendricks,
Crichton Street Public School

Chapter One

Love at First Sight

———

"Mr. Stone?"

"Paul," I said. "Paul Stone."

"I called about your paintings."

"Sure. Come in."

On the phone, she'd said her name was Zena da Silva. Pretty? She was much more than that: she was beautiful. Curves in all the right places. Big, brown eyes. She stepped into the room and looked around, and I fell in love with her. Sure, why not? I think it was the eyes, mainly.

Now those eyes widened and she smiled. "So you really *are* a painter, Mr. Stone."

"What were you expecting?" I said. "Isn't that why you came?" I laughed. I was laughing at myself. Was I really falling in love?

"I meant that you're an artist, that painting is your life."

"Well, I don't paint houses."

Yes, I was an artist. Poor. Struggling. Not quite starving. Painting was my life, but sometimes making a living was hard. My studio was the top floor of an old warehouse. I paid almost no rent, but the water only worked if you knew exactly how to bang on the pipes.

Once, I think, my studio must have been used to store spices. After a heavy rain, the air always smelled of cinnamon and cloves. But it was a great home for a painter. High ceilings. A huge window that filled the room with light. My beautiful visitor had a great view of the paintings I'd leaned against the wall.

I watched Zena as she bent down for a closer look at my work. That was a pleasure, watching her bend down. But don't get the wrong idea. I fell in love because of her eyes. Turning up to me now, they were touched by sadness. And they made an appeal. A call. *Please forgive me*, they said. She was pretending. Faking. Acting a part. *I'm not a bad person underneath*, those big eyes were telling me.

"I like these," she said

She did, too. I could see that. But I could see something else. "You're not going to buy one," I said.

"I'm sorry. I truly would like to." She paused. "I don't know what to say. I'm embarrassed. You see, I really didn't know you were an artist. A true artist, I mean."

"But you came to buy a painting?"

"What I had in mind was a little different. I'm going back to Portugal soon. I am very close to my aunt and uncle there. They live in Lisbon, and my uncle paints as a hobby. I thought I would bring them paintings, pictures of my life in Canada. I have photographs. Could you paint a picture from a photograph?"

"Sure."

Zena glanced down and opened her purse. I think she was glad to look away. She brought out three photographs and handed them to me.

One of the photos was a portrait of Zena, a nice shot showing her head and shoulders.

The second was the shore of a lake—pine trees, birch trees, huge rocks. The third showed three boys playing catch in a park, one wearing a bright red windbreaker. "I took that picture near where I live," she said.

"Really?"

"Yes."

You understand, I didn't believe any of this. I didn't believe her photographs, I didn't believe in her aunt and uncle in Lisbon. But I believed *her*. Not who she was pretending to be but the person she truly was. The person I could see in her eyes. After a moment, I said, "All right. How soon would you want them?"

"In a week. Is that too soon? I want real paintings, oil paintings. One other thing… I already have the frames. I'm sure that is terrible, asking you to paint a picture to fit a frame—" She broke off and looked at me.

"Sure it's terrible. But some people ask me to paint a picture to go with the wallpaper. You have the sizes?"

She went back to her purse. Again, I think she was glad to look away. She had the sizes written on a slip of paper: *60 x 73 centimetres, 60.3 x 72.1 centimetres, 51.3 x 56.5 centimetres.*

"They're not too big?" she asked.

"No, that's fine," I answered.

"Now, you must tell me what they will cost."

"How much do you think would be fair?" I said.

She blushed. "No, no. You must say."

"All right. I say $500 each."

"Yes, good."

"But you should bargain," I said.

Her face turned pink. "You're laughing at me."

"No, I'm not. But you're very pretty when you blush."

She looked away again. When she looked back, her eyes had changed. Something hard had come into them, and I could see how strong she was, how tough. "I will come back for the paintings in a week," she said, "and I will pay you $1,500."

"What's your phone number? I'll call when they're ready."

"No, I'll come back in a week. Next Thursday."

"Where do you live? I can drop them off."

"It's all right," she said. "I don't mind coming. I must thank you, Mr. Stone, you've been very kind."

"Paul," I said. "You should call me Paul."

She hesitated, but then she nodded. "Paul." She held out her hand, and I took it. Small, warm, firm. I liked her hand. I liked her hand and I liked her smile and I liked her eyes, even when they had gone a little hard. She was tough. Strong. Sad. They were all part of who she truly was.

She closed the door behind her. I quickly crossed the room to my big window and watched as she reached the sidewalk and turned up the street.

She didn't want to give me her phone number, or tell me where she lived. Who was she? What was she up to? Two questions. Here was a third: *Who did she think I was?* I'd been a surprise, something she hadn't expected. I'd never seen or heard of her before. How had she heard of me?

I watched as she reached her car, a blue Toyota. She opened the door and slipped inside.

I believed her eyes and her hand, but I didn't believe anything else.

She drove away and was gone, but when I closed my eyes I could see her perfectly.

Like everyone else, you'll think I did this for the money, but you're wrong. I was convinced by those beautiful eyes, from beginning to end.

Chapter Two
Victor, a Crook

———

Three paintings, even small ones, are a lot of work for a week. I started right away.

I began with the landscape. Probably the most famous Canadian painters are the Group of Seven. In the years after the First World War, they hiked and paddled their canoes through northern Ontario, drawing and painting. Zena's photograph reminded me of their pictures, the rugged rocks and the dark shapes of the pine trees, the sun flashing off the waves on a lake. Looking at their paintings, you can almost feel the wind in your face. I did Zena's painting in the same style, broad strokes, full of colour.

Then, Saturday morning, I began on her portrait, from the head-and-shoulders shot she'd given me. It was a beautiful photograph. No, actually. It was a *terrible* photograph, but *she* was beautiful. I took my time. I could see a little sadness in her eyes—even though she was smiling—and I wanted to catch that. What was she sad about? Who was she, really? Why hadn't she wanted me to know where she lived? All the questions I'd asked before flowed through my mind as I worked.

That afternoon, the phone rang, and a few of my questions were answered.

"Dear boy," my caller said. I knew him well: Victor Mellish. "I haven't seen you in weeks. Why don't you drop in? I have a little work for you."

The sign on his store said *Victor Mellish, Antiques.* But the store wasn't really a store, and the "antiques" weren't really antique. They weren't even old. Victor wasn't even a shopkeeper. He didn't sell much of the junk that was piled up behind the dirty window or on the dusty shelves. His shop was full of wobbly chairs, scratched tables, fake gold jewellery, and "vintage fashions" that were just used clothes.

Victor was a merchant, a trader—but what he sold was information. Did you have a fine piece of silver you wanted to sell? Victor would know someone—perhaps even a museum—that wanted to buy it. A rich banker had lost a fortune in the market? Victor would know where he could sell his million-dollar Picasso painting to pay off his debts.

Like any dealer, Victor brought buyers and sellers together, and they paid him a commission for the service. Was he honest? Well, he'd never gone to jail, so he wasn't a criminal. *Not quite.*

He was waiting for me in the back of the store. Behind the scenes, as always.

"What do you think, dear boy? What do you think?"

Victor's little back room held two big leather chairs and a desk that was always covered with books and papers. On a small table sat his hot plate. A kettle was whistling; the air was damp with steam. Victor loved coffee. Now, he bent over the grinder and began grinding the beans, *whirr, whirr, whirr.* "Arabian Midnight," he said, "*very* good." With Victor, there was always some new, fancy blend.

"What do you think?" he murmured again.

The room, lit by one bare bulb in the ceiling, was dark and full of shadows. Stacked against the walls and leaning against the chairs were five of the worst paintings I'd ever seen in my life. They were huge, in heavy frames. A landscape, with trees like green umbrellas and cows like black and white rats. A naked lady dipping her toe in a pool—or at least I thought it was a pool. Perhaps it was a cloud and she was trying to fly. A ship sailing through a storm in a sea that looked like spinach and mashed potatoes. The fourth—but it was too painful to look.

"Where did you find them?" I asked.

Victor turned around. His face was plump and pink, like a baby's. He always wore the same grey suit and grimy white shirt, with a tie knotted like a piece of string. And on top of his head, indoors or out, rain or shine, sat the same shapeless grey hat.

"Halifax," he answered me. "They're all by a dear old businessman. He thought he was a painter, but he was forced into the family firm."

"The family should have pushed harder, I'd say."

"But surely something can be done with them," Victor said. He handed me a cup of coffee. I'll give him credit. The coffee *was* good. "If you put on a layer of varnish, and did some careful re-painting…"

I must now make a confession. Every once and a while, I did a little work for Victor. Even if your rent is low, you have to pay it, right? I'd re-work paintings, Victor would clean up the frames, and they'd become "Old Masters." What is forgery? What is fraud? He wouldn't say that the landscape with the cows that looked like rats was by some famous French artist. He'd only say it was "after" or "in the school of" some famous French artist.

I bent down, studying the paintings more carefully.

"They're filthy," I said. "I'll have to clean them before I can re-paint them."

Victor grunted.

"And they're *big*," I said.

He grunted again.

I stood up. "$300 each."

"Oh dear," said Victor. He eyed me—like a shark eyes a fish. "$250."

"$275."

"Done." And then he added. "How long will it take?"

"I can't do it right away. I've got another rush job."

"Really? So you're busy. How nice."

I looked at him carefully. There was something in his voice, something going on behind that baby pink face. Then I understood.

"Victor," I said, "do you know a girl called Zena da Silva?"

He pursed his lips. "Zena? Da Silva?"

"Victor, a crook like you should be a better liar." All at once, a lot of my questions were answered. How had Zena heard of me? From Victor. Why had she been surprised that I was "a real artist"? Because she was expecting someone like Victor, someone as crooked as he was.

Now, without saying a word, he pressed his face close to mine. I looked into his eyes— small, blue, watery. "Discretion," he said. "It's the first thing you learn in this business."

Discretion. A fancy way of saying, *keep your mouth shut.*

I stared backed at him. "Is that right, Victor?"

"It is, dear boy. Don't you forget it." And his finger tapped hard on my chest.

Chapter Three
Harold Green, Man of the World

———

On Thursday, when Zena picked up the paintings, she looked even more beautiful than she had the week before. And there was that same hint of sadness—but hardness—in her lovely eyes.

"These are very nice, Mr. Stone."

"Paul," I reminded her.

"Yes—Paul. Thank you."

"The portrait, the painting of yourself. Will your aunt and uncle like it?"

"My aunt and uncle—? Oh yes. They will, I'm sure." She looked away. She knew she'd made a slip, a tiny mistake. She opened her purse and took out some bills. "Thank you again."

I took the money. I thought she wanted to say something more, perhaps to explain, but she didn't say anything. I wanted an explanation, too. I would have liked an answer to this question: *How is a girl like you mixed up with a crook like Victor Mellish?* But I was taking Victor's advice and being discreet—keeping my mouth shut. I wrapped up the paintings.

From my big window, I watched as Zena reached the street. I had a decision to make. Was I just going to let her walk out of my life? The answer to that question was easy. *No.* I raced down the stairs.

I don't have a car, but I own a motorcycle, a rusty Suzuki. Like most things in my life, I had to give it a kick, but then it worked. As Zena's car pulled away from the curb, I was right behind her. She led me straight across town and parked in front of an older apartment building, one of those square things, like a Kleenex box. I watched her take the paintings from the back seat of the car and then go inside.

As soon as the door closed, I chased after her. Peering through the door, I saw her get into the elevator. I watched the light above the elevator, and saw that she got off at the fourth floor. But what was I going to do? I didn't know the code to buzz her apartment. Still, I now knew where she lived.

And then, almost by accident, I discovered something else.

As I walked back to my Suzuki, thinking things over, I took a quick glance inside Zena's car. On the shelf behind the back seat, I saw the usual litter: a book of maps, a folding umbrella, a crumpled flyer. *And a glossy catalogue from an art exhibition at the Art Gallery of Ontario.* I leaned closer to the window, shading my eyes with my hand. The exhibition had one of those fancy titles they give art shows: *The Natural Eye: The Painted World.* It was on now.

I hadn't been to the gallery in months. I love art galleries and museums, those marble floors, the echoing halls. I bought a ticket and a copy of the catalogue. A lot of kids were there on a school field trip. They were loving it. But I wasn't sure about their teacher. "No running!" she kept pleading.

I let them get ahead of me and walked slowly past the pictures. Some were by very famous painters: Monet, Pissarro, Turner, Corot. These were the artists the teacher was telling the kids about. But some had been painted by men whose names were not so well known. Three caught my eye:

1. *Florida, Two Hummingbirds*, by Martin Johnson Heade. The birds sparkled like jewels. But what interested me was the size, 60 x 73 centimetres. *Exactly the same size as my painting for Zena of the boys playing ball.*

2. *Jungle Moon*, by Wilfredo Lam. A landscape in his mind, strange, haunting, spooky. Beautiful. My favourite. But what excited me, again, was its size: 51.3 x 56.5 centimetres, *exactly the same as my portrait of Zena.*

3. *Red Lake, Sunset*, by Tom Thomson. The first photograph Zena had given me, the pines and rocks on the lakeshore, had made me think of the Group of Seven painters. Well, Thomson had influenced their work so much that you might call him their artistic father. And I had a little laugh, because my painting, again, was *exactly* the size of his, 60.3 x 72.1 centimetres.

Three paintings, exactly the same size as the paintings I'd done for Zena. Chance? Luck?

Coincidence? I didn't believe it, especially because there was one more coincidence. The three paintings in the exhibition were all owned by the same man. Beside each entry in the catalogue was a little thank-you note: *Kindly loaned by Harold Green, Toronto.*

Harold Green, I suspected, was a rich man. You've never heard of Martin Johnson Heade. Don't be embarrassed, most other people have never heard of him either. He was an American, died in 1904. He painted marshes, beach scenes, flowers, and birds, mostly in Florida. And today one of his hummingbird paintings could be worth $800,000.

Wilfredo Lam? Only art students have heard of him. Still, he is the most important modern painter from Cuba. His best paintings—and the one Harold Green owned was pretty good—sell for around $1,000,000.

That's also what you'd have to pay for a Tom Thomson, at least one as beautiful as the painting Harold Green owned. Together, Harold Green's paintings were worth almost $3,000,000.

Who was Harold Green?

It's a short walk from the Art Gallery of Ontario to the Toronto Public Library. I spent the next two hours there, reading old newspapers and reference books, finding out all I could about Harold Green.

Green had started in the army. Then he'd worked for the government, all over the world, but mostly in the Middle East. He could speak Arabic and also Farsi, the language of Iran. Now he was retired. He divided his time between homes in Toronto, the Bahamas, and Paris. I guessed his money came from his wife, the daughter of a billionaire real-estate developer.

Most of these details came from *Who's Who*, the reference book that tells you everything about important people. But I also read an article on Green and his art collection in the *Toronto Star*. He'd added a modern addition to his big brick house to hold his paintings. He painted, too. In one photo, he was standing beside an easel. "I'm terrible," he had said, "but painting helps me understand and appreciate the real thing."

The real thing. Like the three paintings he'd loaned the gallery, the three paintings Zena was planning to steal.

What else could I think?

Zena and Victor were planning to steal Green's paintings, and somehow *my* three pictures were involved.

Zena the Beautiful; Victor the Crook. I sat back in my chair. How could she do it? "You're crazy!" I blurted out loud.

The librarian turned toward me with a frown and put a finger to her lips. "Shh!"

Chapter Four
Coffee and Crime

You've heard the expression, "running around like a chicken with its head cut off"? That was me for the next few days. I didn't know what to do. I was completely confused. One morning, I went to Zena's apartment building, hoping to catch her as she came out, but she didn't. Next I went around to Victor's shop—but at the last minute I didn't go in. What would I say to him? Then I tried to forget about it. If Zena wanted to do crazy things, that was her business.

But as I told you, this had nothing to do with money; it was all about love. I kept seeing those beautiful eyes! The day the exhibition at the gallery ended, I drove out to Harold Green's place on my motorcycle. I watched the house for an hour. I don't know what I was trying to prove. Rain began to fall. Soon, I was soaked. And to show you how crazy I was, I showed up again the next morning.

But that was more interesting.

The street was quiet, shaded by old maple trees. The big brick house had three stories, with lots of chimneys. At one end, the modern addition stuck out. It was low and made of varnished wood. I knew, from the newspaper story, that this was where Green kept his paintings.

A police car came up the street, a van marked *Security* right behind it. They turned in at Green's house. Two men got out of the van, and a cop got out the car. The door of Green's house opened. With the cop watching, the two men carried the pictures inside: they were being returned from the gallery.

Just then, a car pulled away from the curb, about half a block down from me. A blue Toyota. Zena. She had been watching, too. Of course! They couldn't steal the paintings until they came back from the gallery.

I watched her speed away down the street. She was going too fast for me to catch her, but now I made up my mind. Maybe I was a chicken, maybe I'd lost my head, but I was going to stop running around. I gave the Suzuki a kick and headed for Victor's shop.

Closed.

But I always know where to find Victor. Within three blocks of his place, there's a Starbucks and two other coffee shops. He doesn't usually go to Starbucks. He prefers something special. Today, it was a dark, dim place called the Lively Bean. Ugly booths. Plastic seats. But the room was filled with the wonderful smell of roasting coffee.

Victor was a regular. Instead of a booth, he has his own little table. He was dressed in his usual shapeless hat and grey suit, with a grubby tie knotted around his neck. His watery eyes looked up as I came in. "Paul, dear boy. How lovely to see you."

"Victor, this isn't a social call."

"No? But you'll have some coffee." He waved to the waitress. "Mabel, bring my young friend some of the Jamaican."

As Mabel brought it, I said, "You like to give lectures about discretion. Keeping your mouth shut."

"It's a good habit, my boy."

"Well, I'm going to break it."

"Dear, dear."

"You're going to say this is none of my business, only you made it my business."

Victor sipped his coffee and murmured, "Did I?"

"Admit it. You told Zena to come to me for those paintings."

"Perhaps I did." He put his cup down and looked at me, straight on. "Which is why I've been expecting to see you."

"What do you mean?"

"I knew you'd catch on."

"But you've fooled Zena."

Victor laughed. "I don't think so. Paul, the beautiful Zena is far from a fool."

"Victor, I don't want her mixed up with you."

He laughed again. "Dear boy, I believe you're in love with her. You should see your face. Such passion! You're going to save this beautiful lady from wicked old *me*!"

"Something like that," I said.

"Well, you've got it wrong. And there are other values in life besides love. Money counts for something, surely."

"Victor, you know all about that."

"So does your beautiful friend," Victor replied. "I hope it won't shock you to learn that this was entirely her idea. I'm not involving her in anything, she involved *me*. If you don't believe it, ask her yourself."

He looked up.

I turned around. Zena had come in. She was wearing a light grey suit, and her hair was pulled back from her face. She looked like the most beautiful businesswoman in the world.

"Hello, Mr. Stone," she said. And then she smiled. "Hello, Paul, I mean."

Victor murmured beside me. "She involved me, dear boy. Now we want to involve you."

Chapter Five
I Sign On

———

"The moment I saw you," Zena said, "I knew you were perfect."

The moment I saw *you*, I thought, I knew you were perfect, too. But I only thought this, keeping my mouth shut. Victor would approve; I was being discreet. But then I did ask, "Perfect for what?"

When she smiled, she had dimples, two sweet little hollows in her cheeks. She glanced quickly at Victor. "Well," she said, "I knew it would be easier with three."

Victor took a sip of his coffee, then set it down. "Zena is being polite, for my sake. It's a question of my physical abilities. You are a good deal younger, stronger, fitter. Those qualities will be a help in our little job."

"You're crazy. You want me to hit someone over the head?"

Victor laughed. "No, no, dear boy. Nothing like that. You shock me. Surely you know me better."

I was a little surprised, to tell you the truth. Victor was no angel, but violence wasn't his line. "Then you better explain," I said.

I looked at Zena. It was a great pleasure to look at Zena. This close, I could even smell her perfume: light, spicy. I wanted to press my face in her hair and—I resisted. "Why don't you start at the beginning?" I said.

She began to talk in a low, quick voice. She'd gone to work for Harold Green as his secretary when Green was writing a book. "It was about peace," she said. "What a two-faced liar he is! A hypocrite! All he really cares about is being rich." As she'd worked for him, she'd learned the routine of his house, and how the paintings were guarded.

"Wait," I said. "Back up a moment. How did you meet Green?"

"I was born in Iran—well, we still like to think of it as Persia. I speak Farsi, the language of Persia, and so does Green, but he can't write Farsi. He wanted a person who could."

"Did you live there? In the house?"

"No, but sometimes I did stay overnight." She looked at me. "No, it's not what you think." From the look on her face, I knew it wasn't. For some reason, she hated Harold Green. I was curious. Why?

"If the paintings are stolen," I asked, "won't he think of you?"

"No. Not if we make it look like an ordinary art theft. Don't people steal paintings? Yes, all the time. Besides, I'm a woman. Harold Green wouldn't think a woman could be strong enough to do such a thing."

"Okay, so how *can* you do it?"

She leaned closer to me. She put her hand over mine. That made listening hard, but I did my best. "The whole house is protected by alarms. But they are only turned on at night, at 11:30. The alarms are turned on by a computer in Green's study, the room where he works. When I was with him, that's where I used to work, too. I saw everything."

"But how can you stop the alarms coming on?"

"Simple. Like all computers, this one has a clock. Before 11:30, you simply set the clock back. Then everything will *seem* to be normal, you see."

Victor looked at me. "You see how smart this young lady is?"

"All right, but to get to the computer you have to get into the house—"

"Every night, the man who looks after the house—the butler—takes the garbage out to a shed. His name is Bellows. He likes to smoke cigars, but he can't in the house. It's bad for the paintings. All over the house are smoke detectors. So, every night, Bellows takes out the garbage and smokes a cigar. Of course, he has to come back inside before 11:30, before the computer sets the alarms. But we can slip in ahead of him and change the clock. Then, he will come back in and go to bed, and we can take the paintings."

Victor said, "I watched him one night. He walks away from the house and behind the shed. If you're quick, you'll be able to go in the back door. He won't see you. The next part is more difficult. That's where you come in. I was going to do it, but you'll do it *much* better."

I took a sip of my coffee. "So what's this difficult part?"

Zena leaned toward me. "The computer runs the house alarms. But each of the paintings has its own alarm, built into its hanger on the wall. These alarms work on a spring. If you take the painting away—remove its weight—the spring moves up and the alarm goes off. So here's what we'll do. We'll slip a loop of wire over the painting so it catches on the hanger. Then we'll run this loop to a turnbuckle, a gadget invented for exactly this job: tightening wires. We'll attach the turnbuckle to an eye bolt we'll screw into the floor. By twisting on the turnbuckle, we'll tighten the wire so it pulls down on the spring. When it's pulling down with the same weight as the painting, we can take the painting away."

I thought about it. "All right. That might work. You'd have to do it very carefully."

"Indeed, dear boy," said Victor. "It will take young nerves and muscles, and yours are so much younger than mine. That's why we need you—if I did it, those alarms would be ringing so loudly they'd wake the dead."

I wanted a moment to think things over. I was really thinking about Zena, asking myself the question, *what is she really up to?* But I looked at Victor and said, "Okay, Victor, I supply steady nerves and young muscle. What's your contribution? How do you earn your share?"

He leaned forward, folding his hands in front of him. "Well, when you talk about shares—money—you are certainly coming around to me. Think. We have the paintings, but we want to change them into money. We could try to sell them, of course, but that would be dangerous. Soon, every gallery and museum and police force, all over the world, will have photographs of those paintings. But Harold Green is a careful man. Those paintings are insured… for how much, do you think?"

"I'd guess $3,000,000."

"A very good guess, I expect. So, if the paintings are stolen, Green will claim $3,000,000 from the insurance company. But I'll arrange to sell them back to the company for only $600,000. We'll split it three ways, $200,000 each. The insurance company will be delighted, truly happy. They won't have to pay the $3,000,000 claim, only our—shall we say, our fee? Even Harold Green should be pleased. He'll get his paintings back. The only person who might be unhappy is Bellows, the butler. I'm afraid he may take a certain amount of the blame."

"Victor, you're such a sensitive fellow, to worry about him."

Victor smiled. "What do you say?"

"I'd like a little time to think about it."

"Harold Green is in Paris. We should do it before he comes back."

"And when is that?" I asked.

"Friday."

"Today's Wednesday!"

Victor raised his eyebrow. "Are you busy tomorrow night?"

Zena squeezed my hand. I looked into those eyes… those eyes! I keep telling you, it had nothing to do with the money…

"Mabel," Victor called to the waitress. "Bring us another cup, if you would."

But I wanted something stronger than coffee… rye whiskey, perhaps.

Chapter Six
Break-in

10:00 p.m. A dark night, with no moon.

I crouched down in the lilac bushes behind Green's house. A breeze rustled through the leaves. Far off, I could hear the rumble of traffic and, beside me, the soft rise and fall of Zena's breathing.

She wore blue jeans, a grey sweater, black Nikes. As beautiful as ever—that sweater was wonderfully tight. She carried a big cloth bag filled with the tools we'd need to fool the alarms on the paintings. I was wearing jeans and a black jacket. In the darkness, we were almost invisible.

"He won't be long now," Zena whispered.

Actually, Bellows didn't appear until 10:42. A light came on over the back door, and he backed through it, lugging two plastic bags of garbage. He was a tall, old guy with a stoop. He went up the narrow walk to a little shed, and a sliding door rumbled open. Zena put her hand on my arm. "Wait," she hissed.

She was right. Bellows went back into the house and came out again, with two more bags. He tossed them into the shed and then slid the door shut. A moment later, a match flared. I had a quick glimpse of his face, bent down to the light. Then I could smell his cigar.

He walked slowly away, through the garden, enjoying his smoke. Soon, all I could see was the red tip of his cigar. Then even that disappeared.

Zena nudged me. We ran softly toward the door. Here was the real moment of danger. The light over the door wasn't bright, but if Bellows looked back, he might see us.

He didn't.

We slipped through.

We were in a dark room with a tiled floor. Zena led the way—she knew where she was going, and she had a little flashlight.

We tiptoed upstairs, into a hall. Here, the lights were on. Zena took my arm. "This way."

We stepped through a door. In this room, the lights were off. Zena quickly flashed her light into the dark. A big room, set up like an office. Desk. File cabinets. Two big leather chairs—they gleamed black in the light. Zena stepped behind the desk, but she didn't sit down. Smart. A chair might creak. Leaning forward, she tapped a key on the keyboard. The computer screen lit up. She whispered, "You see, it is always on."

I was worried about the light from the screen, but Zena was quick. She found the menu for "Clock Set." I looked at my watch. 11:05. She set the time back to 10:00. At 11:30, when the alarms were supposed to come on, the computer would think there was more than an hour to go.

"Come," Zena said, "I'll show you where we can hide."

She led me to the back of Green's office. Here, she pushed against a folding door. We stepped into a small storeroom, its shelves piled high with paper and boxes of office supplies.

How long did we sit there? Forever. I strained my ears. Finally, I heard a door close somewhere, and Zena whispered, "That is Bellows. He always tests the front door and bangs it shut before he locks it. Now he'll go up to his room, on the third floor."

It was 11:25. As far as Bellows knew, the alarms would come on in five minutes. We gave him ten. Then Zena pushed the door open and we stepped back into the office. Bellows had turned out all the lights in the house and closed the curtains. I suppose that's how he kept the house when Green was away. It was really dark. I kept one hand on Zena's shoulder. Twice, I hit my knees against tables or chairs, but we didn't knock anything over. Green's special gallery was at the far end of house. I was glad when we finally reached it.

A fan hummed softly, keeping the air dry for the paintings. Zena flashed the light around, but kept it low, on the floor. The room was shaped like a shoebox. I could see that Green's paintings were on the long back wall. The windows along the front wall were covered by heavy drapes—strong sunlight hurts paintings.

An easel and a table with tin cans full of brushes and palette knives, and twisted tubes of old paint, stood against the shorter outside wall. I remembered that Green liked to paint. But he hadn't painted the pictures in his gallery. Very impressive. I almost whistled. I counted them. Eighteen. And at least a dozen were worth stealing, though the three we wanted were certainly the best.

Zena picked them out with her light: Heade's *Hummingbirds*, Wilfredo Lam's *Jungle*, and Tom Thomson's *Red Lake.*

Now came the tricky part. I took the flashlight from Zena. Kneeling down, I shone the light up behind the frame of the hummingbird painting. I could see the glint of the wire attached to the painting where it passed over the hanger.

Zena took one of the wire loops out of her bag. I drilled a little hole in the floor, then screwed an eye bolt into it. I then looped the wire over the painting until I felt it catch on the hanger.

"Be careful," said Zena.

I was. Gently, I attached the end of the wire to the turnbuckle, then hooked the turnbuckle to the screw eye in the floor. My hands were sweating as I tightened the turnbuckle. One turn… another… tighter… tighter… This sounds complicated, but it worked just like a necktie around a man's neck. I was pulling down on the long end of the tie.

At a certain point, I was pulling down with the same force as the weight of the painting. Take the painting away, and the alarm on the hanger wouldn't know the difference… I hoped.

"Be careful!" Zena hissed again.

I took hold of the frame. Steady nerves, as Victor had said. Were mine steady enough? I lifted the painting free of the hanger…

No ringing bells…

No flashing lights…

But I was sure holding my breath.

"You did it!"

"I think you should kiss me," I said.

"All right!"

"And one kiss each for the other two?"

"Hurry up!"

The other two were easier. Soon, the last of them, Tom Thomson's *Red Lake*, was in my hand. Zena held her big cloth bag open toward me.

"My kiss?"

"Don't be silly, Paul!"

"I'm not being silly."

"There," she murmured, a moment later. "Now we have to get out of here."

We tiptoed out of the room, leaving the wires behind. Stretched between the screw eyes in the floor and the hangers on the wall, they looked like strange musical instruments.

We reached the hall outside Green's office. My eyes were used to the dark and I could see the stairs as we went down to the back door. One creak. We stepped carefully. In a few seconds, we were outside.

Zena grabbed my arm. "Wait!"

"What is it?"

"In his study, by the computer—I was fiddling with my ring. I left it there!"

"You're crazy!"

"I have to get it! It has my name inside!"

I looked at my watch. "Zena, the alarms come back on in three minutes."

"Stay here. I have time."

Before I could stop her, she ducked inside. What was she doing? I stared at the second hand

47

on my watch. Two minutes… one minute… thirty seconds…

With eight seconds to go, Zena opened the door and came out.

"I found it!" she said. Her cheeks were flushed, and she was breathing fast. Which looked really good, in that tight sweater. But for the moment I wasn't thinking about her tight sweater, not even about her kisses.

We found Victor, parked down the block. He saw Zena's bulging bag and started the engine. "Well done," he said. "How did it go?"

I looked at Zena—who was looking straight ahead out the window. "Fine," I said, "until right at the end."

Victor stared at me, frowning. "What happened?"

Keep your mouth shut. Be discreet. What had happened? I didn't know… but I wished I did.

Chapter Seven
Moving House

———

Maybe you're wondering what happened to the three paintings I'd originally painted for Zena, the reason I was mixed up in all this. Well, the answer was revealed the next morning, in Zena's apartment.

Think. As soon as the robbery was discovered, police all over the world would be looking for those paintings. Where could we hide them? We needed them to be easy to get at. That way, Victor could move quickly when he sold them back to the insurance company.

Victor's solution was clever. After the robbery, we took my paintings—exactly the same size, remember—and stretched them over the paintings we'd stolen from Green. We put my kids playing catch over the hummingbirds. My portrait of Zena went over Wilfredo Lam's jungle. And my picture of a rocky lakeshore had the honour of covering Tom Thomson's painting of Red Lake.

The next morning, movers showed up, cheerful fellows with lots of muscle. Drinking our coffee, we watched them pack the paintings, and Zena's other stuff, into cardboard boxes. Then they loaded the boxes into a van to move her to Los Angeles.

Brilliant. How were the police going to find the paintings in the middle of a move across the continent? My only question was, why L.A.?

"Why not?" said Victor. "Green's insurance company has offices everywhere. Some criminals may prefer to return to the scene of the crime. I'd prefer to be as far away as possible. Besides, I know Los Angeles rather well. We give the insurance fellows the paintings, they give us the money. Sounds simple, but it will be rather tricky, I think." His watery eyes widened and he smiled. "Everything depends on the exchange."

"Sure, Victor. That's how we get our money. But stay out of jail."

"You're such a bright boy," he said. "Here's your ticket."

We flew on separate planes. Victor had even reserved rooms for us in three separate hotels. On the plane, I slept. When I woke up, I began thinking. All my questions about Zena came back. She hated Green, I was sure. What was she up to? And what had happened at the last minute, when she'd run back into the house?

I also had questions about Victor. I looked out the window as we passed over long, sandy wastes of the American desert. Los Angeles. There was something suspicious about this trip. L.A. isn't a centre for the insurance business. It's not even a centre for the art world. So what was Victor up to? Was he playing a trick? Pulling a fast one?

Victor called me in my hotel that night. "I have appointed myself social director, camp counsellor, and your chief guide. Let us meet for breakfast, at my hotel, at nine."

Victor was all smiles the next morning. He had found a store that sold the Toronto papers. "We don't even rate a line," he said.

"It's too early," said Zena. Without asking permission, I'd given her a kiss as I'd sat down.

"Perhaps," Victor replied. "But the robbery may not have been reported to the police." He smiled. "The police will want to catch us and serve the interests of justice. But the insurance company won't be so moral. They may have told Green to keep quiet, knowing that they might be able to buy the paintings back from us. We may have some breathing room."

"Don't count on it," I said.

"Oh, I don't. That's what I want to talk about, in fact. How are we going to get away with this? Each of us must make separate plans, but even apart we are still linked. If one of us is caught, surely we all will be."

Victor reached inside his old grey suit and brought out two envelopes, placing one in front of me, the other in front of Zena. "Of course, I will tell the insurance company to give us our money in old bills. But the bills will certainly be marked. In the envelopes in front of you, you'll find $10,000. Surely that will meet your immediate needs. For a time you won't have to touch the insurance money at all."

It was Zena who smiled. "You are so thoughtful, Victor. This will give *you* more breathing room, all right. By the time Paul and I begin spending the marked money, you will be far, far away."

"Africa," Victor said. "South America. China. There's so much of the world I still haven't seen."

Late the next afternoon, we met again. Victor had rented a car. He drove us out to the storage lockers where the movers would deliver Zena's stuff including the paintings. She picked up her locker key at the desk.

"I think I should take the paintings when they get here," Victor said.

It made sense. In working out the deal with the insurance company, he'd need to be able to get the paintings quickly.

"Okay, Victor," I said, "but don't get any fancy ideas."

He dropped me at my hotel. Since he had a car, I decided to rent one as well. After all, we were in Los Angeles, home of the freeway. A taxi took me to the nearest Hertz office and I rented a Ford. Twenty minutes later, as I pulled out of the lot, I glanced into my rear-view mirror. There was Zena, climbing into a rented car herself!

I pulled over to the curb and waited. As she came out of the Hertz lot, I trailed her. She followed the signs and drove straight to the airport. She parked, I parked. She went in, I followed. She went up to a ticket counter, I stayed back, so she wouldn't see me. She paid cash, I suppose with some of Victor's money. When she left, I went up to the counter.

"I was thinking of a trip," I said.

The woman laughed. "Sounds like a good idea to me. Where to?"

I threw a glance toward Zena as she walked away. "Maybe where that gorgeous girl's going."

"Lisbon? Portugal?" The woman laughed again. "Won't do you any good. She bought two tickets, so she must be going with somebody else."

Lisbon. Well, that's where she was from. I'd been suspicious so long I was almost surprised that Zena had told the truth. And I was upset. I didn't want to lose her. Turning away from the counter, I ran after her but by the time I reached the parking lot, her car was pulling away.

Then, the next day, my suspicions turned back to Victor. We met for dinner. Everyone was tense. The paintings arrived the next day. After that came the exchange with the insurance company. Except for the robbery, this would be the most dangerous moment of all.

"You must trust me," said Victor.

"That's exactly the problem," I said.

"Zena isn't worried, are you my dear?" Victor turned to me. "At the end, she will have the money, and it is you who will hand over the paintings. I will only make the arrangements."

Victor said he'd already told the insurance company we had the paintings, and now he told us how he'd work the exchange. The problem, of course, was that talking to the company gave them a chance to find us. They could trace his phone calls. "But I'll use three separate cell phones," he said. "I'll put those little cards you can buy in a smoke shop into them. I will only make one call from each phone, and I'll be in my car, driving. So they can trace each call, but I'll already be gone, and my next call will be on a different phone, from a different place." He laid out his three shiny new cell phones in front of him.

A few minutes later, I left to go to the washroom. On the way, I passed the rack where we had hung our coats—it had been raining outside. I suppose cell phones were on my mind. Victor's coat hung on the rack like a limp dishrag, and I saw where the pocket bulged. I looked back. A big post blocked the view from our table; Victor couldn't see me. I slipped my hand into the pocket of his coat and felt the old cell phone he normally used. Taking it, I ducked into the washroom.

I pressed Recent Calls.

Nine calls had been made to someone called "T. Crowder" at a number here, in Los Angeles.

T. Crowder? Who could he be?

There was an easy way to find out. I pushed Call.

From the washroom, the signal was pretty weak, but the phone started ringing. A female voice answered. "The Crowder residence. Good evening."

"Is that Mrs. Crowder?"

"No, sir. It's Maria, the maid."

"Thank you."

I pushed End Call.

T. Crowder, it seemed, was rich enough to live in a "residence" rather than a house. He could also afford a maid.

On my way back to the table, I slipped the phone back into Victor's coat pocket. I was smiling as I sat down. All my questions, I thought, had been answered. *Victor*, I said to myself, *what a wicked fellow you are.*

Chapter Eight
Dollars for Art

———

Victor's exchange plan was a scam, a big lie. I'll give him credit, though—it *sounded* good, it *looked* good.

Supposedly, Victor was driving all over Los Angeles, talking to the insurance company. Supposedly, he was telling them where they should take the money and where they should pick up the paintings. This way, he said, when we picked up the money, we wouldn't be picked up ourselves by the police. All that stuff with the cell phones made the story convincing. But in fact, I felt pretty sure Victor was sitting in some coffee shop, reading his newspapers.

Why didn't I say anything?

I was taking Victor's advice, keeping my mouth shut, being discreet. He was playing a game. I was playing along. Winning, for me, meant staying out of jail... and Zena. My share of $600,000? I told you in the beginning, I didn't care about the money at all.

Victor's game ended in Los Angeles, in Union Station. It's the old train station, which opened in 1939. You can see it in black and white movies. The outside is like a Mexican palace, with a huge clock tower. To one side, there's a beautiful garden. Inside, the tile floors have patterns like Navajo Indian rugs. Some of the ceilings are as high as a five-storey building. As for the trains, you can travel from here to anywhere in the United States, or you can just go across Los Angeles on the Metro Rail lines.

The next afternoon, at two o'clock, I was sitting in a big padded leather chair in the station's waiting room. Beside me was a suitcase. Victor had given it to me. It was locked with a combination lock. Inside were the paintings.

I was sitting on the left side of the waiting room.

Zena was also sitting in one of those comfortable chairs, over on the right side. I couldn't quite see her.

At 2:14 a tall man with short grey hair walked down the centre of the hall. Wearing a blue business suit and a tan raincoat, he pulled a red suitcase behind him. He looked around, stopped beside the ninth seat on the right-hand side, and sat down. Two minutes later, he stood up and casually walked away without the suitcase. A minute after that, Zena appeared. Without stopping, she took the suitcase… and the $600,000 in it. Pulling the suitcase behind her, Zena walked away, down the hall. She gave me a look—and one little smile.

Was it a trap? Were the police going to jump out and arrest her? Victor said no—because we still had the paintings. Zena was now out of my sight, but I knew where she was going. She would head through the station to the Metro Rail platform. She'd board a Gold Line train and ride to the next stop on the line, Chinatown. There, she'd get off and walk to the Thien Hau Temple. The temple was one of the important sights in Chinatown. Crowds of tourists would be all around it, snapping pictures.

Victor had arranged for a taxi to pick Zena up at the temple and take her to a fancy hotel, the Beverly Hills. After all this, if Zena was sure she hadn't been followed, she was to telephone me. Then I would put my suitcase, holding the paintings, on a train to San Diego. Someone from the insurance company would pick up my suitcase there.

Complicated? Sure. But the train to San Diego takes two and a half hours. Even if the company called the police after they got the suitcase, we'd have lots of time to get away.

That's what we were supposed to do. Except it was all a game, a scam—Victor's scam. And I'd decided to stop playing along.

As soon as Zena disappeared, I arose from my comfortable chair. Carrying my suitcase, I walked over to the information counter.

"I'd like to page someone," I said.

"What name, sir?"

"T. Crowder."

"*T*. Crowder?"

"I don't know his first name."

"Okay, anything you say."

A moment later, the public address system came on with a crackle. "T. Crowder... T. Crowder... would T. Crowder meet his party at the information counter."

I stepped back from the counter.

Two minutes later, a man hurried up. He was dressed in a tan raincoat and a blue business suit; his hair was grey and cut very short. It was the man who'd been pulling the suitcase, no doubt about it. Now, he looked very worried.

"Mr. Crowder?" I said.

For a second, he wasn't sure he wanted to admit it. Then he frowned and said, "Yes, I'm Thomas Crowder."

"It's okay, Mr. Crowder, I'm not a policeman."

His expression grew even more worried. "A policeman?"

"That's right. I'm *not* a policeman... just like you're not from an insurance company. Of course," I added, "it *is* a crime, receiving art works and knowing them to be stolen."

"I don't know what you're talking about."

"Wasn't that you, pulling the suitcase? The red one? With $600,000 in it?"

His eyes narrowed. "What's your game?" he said.

"No, no. You're playing the game. Maybe we should go over here and talk about it."

Thomas Crowder was frightened. For a moment, he thought of running away—I could see it in his eyes. But I held up the suitcase with the paintings in it, and he followed me.

When we were back in the waiting room— sitting in those comfortable, padded chairs—I set the suitcase on my lap, across my knees. I fiddled with the combination lock and said, "I only want to get a few things straight. In your pocket, you have a ticket to San Diego."

"Perhaps I do."

"When you got off the train, you were going to pick up this suitcase. And of course you know the combination to the lock."

He licked his lips nervously. "You seem to know everything."

"Not *quite* everything," I said. "That's why I want you to open the suitcase."

"What if I refuse?"

"I won't give it to you." I sat back. "Mr. Crowder, I don't think you're going to call the police and complain that somebody stole your nice red suitcase with $600,000 in it." I tapped my suitcase with my finger. "If you want what you paid for, you'll have to open this up."

He licked his lips again, but then he nodded.

I held the suitcase toward him but kept both hands on it as he worked the lock.

When the lock popped open, I lifted the lid. *Two* paintings, neatly wrapped, lay inside. I smiled. "Well, well," I said.

"Yes," said Crowder. "And I've paid for them."

"So you have. The Wilfredo Lam… and the two hummingbirds?"

"Yes, damn you. Give that case to me."

I held it out to him—but kept hold of the handle. "One thing more, Mr. Crowder. Do you know what discretion means? Do you know how to be discreet?"

"I suppose I do."

I'm a nice guy, don't you think? But the look I gave Crowder wasn't so nice. "Keep your mouth shut. Don't call Victor. *Don't*. That way, you'll have no trouble from me."

He nodded and took the case. Down the hall, two old ladies were hurrying along. "Come on, Ethel, come *on*! We'll miss our train." I watched Thomas Crowder pass through the crowd. He was going home to his "residence," where his maid, Maria, would probably bring him a drink. When he was gone, I walked out of the station and found a taxi to take me to Victor's hotel.

Chapter Nine
Victor Talks

———

Victor wasn't in his room.

I should have guessed.

At the front desk, I asked, "Is there a coffee house near the hotel? Not a Starbucks, something special. Maybe an older place…"

The clerk frowned but then broke into a smile. "You must mean the Last Drop!"

I found the Last Drop two blocks away. Victor was sitting at a table by himself, newspapers spread all around him. He frowned as I came over.

"It's okay," I said, sitting down. "Mr. Crowder has his paintings."

His expression was blank, then furious. "I see."

"No, Victor, *I* see."

He grunted. "You're such a bright boy, Paul."

"We came to Los Angeles because this is where Crowder lives. You never intended to do a deal with the insurance company, did you?"

"No, no. That would have been much too dangerous. We certainly would have been caught."

"Besides," I said, "you're a *dealer*. You bring buyer and seller together. There was something to sell. You knew who wanted to buy."

"Exactly." He brightened. "And like all dealers, I try to create satisfaction, good feeling. True, Harold Green has lost his paintings. But he will receive $3,000,000 from the insurance company. Thomas Crowder has long wanted paintings by those great artists. Now he has them, and at a very cheap price. As for us, well, $200,000 each is a reasonable fee, don't you think? So, you see—something for everyone."

I rested my hand on my chin and stared at him, slowly shaking my head. "Victor, I made Crowder open the suitcase. *Two* paintings. You sold him only *two* paintings. You kept the third one, the Tom Thomson, for yourself. I suppose you've lined up a buyer? Back in Toronto?"

When people smile, they show their teeth. But a dog shows its teeth when it snarls. Victor's smile was a snarl. "What if I have?"

"How much is he willing to pay?"

"$50,000."

"Victor, do you really expect me to believe that? The Tom Thomson is a great painting and has to be worth—"

"All right, all right," he interrupted. "$300,000. Cash."

"Good. You keep that for yourself. Zena and I will split the $600,000 from Crowder. Equal shares."

"That is hardly fair. For one thing, I advanced each of you $10,000."

I waved my hand. "Okay, we'll pay you back."

Now his smile was really a smile. "Do you think you can speak for your beautiful lady friend?"

His tone was mocking, making fun of me. "What do you mean, Victor?"

"You think you're so smart, Paul."

"I'm smart enough. Smart enough to figure out your little scam."

"Yes, but have you figured out the beautiful Zena's? Haven't you felt, all along, that our mysterious lady was up to something, playing a game of her own?"

I didn't say anything. Of course, he was right. From the very first time I'd seen her, I'd guessed that something was going on that I didn't understand. Who was she? What was she doing? How had she become involved with Victor Mellish? Why had she become a thief? Why did she hate Harold Green? With Zena, I'd only ever had questions… and adored those wonderful eyes.

Just then, my phone buzzed in my pocket. I pulled it out.

"Paul? This is Zena. Everything is all right. No one followed me."

She believed Victor, she was still playing *his* game. But I knew Victor was right. She was playing a game of her own.

"It's okay," I said.

"So what should I do? You will give them the paintings?"

"Sure," I said, "don't worry."

I think she heard something in my voice because now she was silent. Then she said, "Is everything all right?"

"Yes. Just go back to your hotel."

Another silence. Then, "You're sure, Paul?"

"Yes." And then, before she could break off, I added, "Zena, I know about Lisbon. I know you're leaving."

"But that's not until later tonight. I'll see you at my hotel."

I ended the call. Victor grunted. "Lisbon? Tonight? We'll have to hurry." He laughed. "You've had a surprise for me, now maybe I'll have one for you." He quickly drained his coffee cup. Victor never forgot his coffee. "Come along, dear boy. My car is outside."

Chapter Ten
The Truth about Zena

———

Zena's hotel was in Santa Monica, a pretty part of Los Angeles. Palm trees line the streets, and beautiful girls walk on the beach as the Pacific surf rolls in. In the summer, the breeze is cool and the sky is blue—but you've seen it on TV.

The hotel was old. The elevator was tiny. Going up to Zena's room, I was jammed tight against Victor. Something hard dug into my leg. "What's that?" I said.

The door opened and we stepped out. "This?" said Victor, reaching into his pocket. "This is a pistol. As you see, I am now pointing it at you. Please. The lovely Zena's room is that way."

He motioned with the gun. And one look at his face told me that he might use it. This was a new Victor, one I'd never seen before.

I went up to Zena's door and knocked. Victor was right behind me. As the door opened, he pushed hard against my back and I staggered in. By the time I found my balance, he had closed the door and was leaning back against it, the gun still in his hand.

Zena had backed up against the bed. Three suitcases were piled on top of it. The red one, from Crowder. And two others—packed and closed. "What's going on?" Zena said.

Victor waved the gun, motioning me to move away. He looked at Zena. "You know perfectly well what's going on." He smiled. "Are you going somewhere? Lisbon? I'll just relieve you of some of your luggage."

"I brought the money," she said. "There it is!"

"Well, we might as well start with that," Victor said. "Open it."

"But there's a lock, a combination."

I said, "Victor will tell you what is, won't you, Victor?"

"So I will. Twenty-six. Fourteen. Three. You line the numbers up with the white mark." Zena looked at me, and I nodded. She turned to the suitcase. As she worked the lock, Victor kept talking. "I won't bore you with all the details, Paul. I was always suspicious. She calls herself Zena da Silva, a perfectly good Portuguese name, but I was curious. She speaks Farsi, the language of Persia… Iran, as it is today. I have a friend, a dreadful man who picks pockets and steals purses. I told him I wanted to know what was in this young lady's purse. But he must on no account steal it. What he found was a passport, Portuguese, in the name of Zena Jafari. That is a name from Iran, and I recognized it." He stopped himself. Zena had opened the suitcase. "Let us see," Victor said. "Let us see."

Zena emptied the contents of the suitcase onto the bed—bundles of hundred dollar bills.

Victor turned to me. "I think, if you count it, you'll find $600,000. As I told you. I've kept my end of the bargain. You can take your shares."

"So why the gun?"

He smiled at me, but his eyes flicked back to Zena. "You've been so suspicious of me, Paul. What about her? Did you have no suspicions at all?"

I was watching him carefully. And I was certainly watching the gun. "I had questions," I said.

"*Questions*. A more polite word. And let me answer your question about the gun. As I said, I'm going to be taking some of this lady's luggage. Not one of the suitcases, I think. What I want is very small." He smiled at Zena. "You'd want to keep them with you, so where is your carry-on bag?"

Zena's eyes gave her away. She darted a glance toward a large purse, beside the bed. "Ah," said Victor, seeing it. He turned to me. "What we took from Harold Green was worth a few hundred thousand to us. What's in that purse is worth millions. Zena, you see, was planning her own little robbery. We helped her get into the house and we gave her cover, but she wanted something else. Four tiny Persian paintings, miniatures, perfect works of art. These are especially rare, by the great master, Reza Abbasi."

Now Zena cried out, "They are mine! They belong to my family! Green made us sell them for nothing, in return for papers to get out of Iran!"

Victor looked at me, "She's telling the truth, for once. Jafari. I told you I recognized the name. Her father. He had a great collection of Persian art, and these were his prize pieces. They were so valuable and so well known that Green didn't dare show them. If he did, people would know that he had stolen them. But you knew where they were, didn't you, Zena?"

So that was why Zena had run back into Green's house.

"Yes," Zena said. "I saw him hide them once, in a hidden place in the wall." She looked at me. "He's right, I needed you to help me break into the house. If they were taken as part of a bigger robbery, he wouldn't think of me, or at least not right away." Then, gripping the handle of her purse, she turned to Victor. "These are mine. They are my birthright. They are my father's soul, and they are the soul of my family."

"Are they, dear? That may all be true—but this is a gun."

Victor stepped toward Zena, but with a flick of her wrist she threw the bag at him. The gun went off. I dove, low and hard, at Victor's legs. We both went down. I saw the gun by my foot and kicked it toward the bed. I sprang to my feet.

Victor got up slowly, and I turned around. Zena had her purse in one hand—and the gun in the other. She smiled. "Now," she said, "I have the gun."

She levelled it. Her hand was perfectly steady.

Victor looked at me. "You think you're so smart. You think she's going to shoot me. But I'm afraid she's going to shoot both of us and then take off for Lisbon."

I smiled at Zena. "But you bought *two* tickets," I said.

"You knew? Well, I was going to ask if you'd like to come with me."

I nodded at Victor. "What are we going to do about him?"

Zena shrugged. "You decide."

"Okay," I said. I gave Victor a smile as I drew back my arm. My knuckles hurt for a week.

Chapter Eleven
The Persian Miniatures

I told you in the beginning, all this had nothing to do with the money. Actually, we left most of it with Victor, and of course he also had the Tom Thomson painting to sell. No, Zena had what she wanted, the miniatures, and I had what I wanted—her.

So we flew off to Lisbon, wondering if the police would come looking for us. But they didn't.

As for the miniatures, they were beautiful. They were delicate, graceful, haunting. Ancient princes and their ladies, magical landscapes, flowering trees, strange birds. I'm a painter, and let me tell you—that Abbasi guy was good.

In Portugal, Zena and I went down to the sea and rented a cottage. One morning, I set the miniatures up on the windowsill, where they caught the sunlight. They looked like pictures of heaven.

Maybe that was the morning we started thinking, who did they really belong to?

Harold Green would have said they were his, and maybe a court would have agreed. Zena's father was dead. Though she'd promised, on his deathbed, to get them back, now she wasn't sure she'd done the right thing. She had the miniatures, but they didn't bring her father back.

We looked at them, sitting on the windowsill. "Only we can see them," she said, "that's the trouble. They belong to everyone, all over the world."

A week later, I wiped the miniatures very carefully to get rid of any fingerprints and wrapped them up. Then Zena took them to the post office and sent them to a great art gallery. I hope you won't mind if I'm discreet once again and don't mention its name. Two weeks later, a little item appeared in the *Times* of London.

An unknown person has given the museum four Persian miniatures by Reza Abbasi, the greatest artist of his time. The works had once belonged to the famous collector Hamid Jafari. For many years, they were believed to be lost. John Morton, the museum's Persian art specialist, said that finding them is a "miracle." Asked how much they are worth, Mr. Morton shook his head. "I can't guess at their value," he said. "They are priceless."

When I read this to Zena, she asked me, "What do you think? Are they truly priceless? Can any work of art be *priceless*?"

"Come over here," I said.

She came over and stood beside me. I drew her to me and kissed her softly.

"Whatever the miniatures are worth," I said, "that was worth a lot more."

Good 🕮 Reads

Discover Canada's Bestselling Authors with Good Reads Books

Good Reads authors have a special talent—
the ability to tell a great story, using clear language.

Good Reads books are ideal for people

✳ on the go, who want a short read;
✳ who want to experience the joy of reading;
✳ who want to get into the reading habit.

To find out more, please visit
www.GoodReadsBooks.com

～⌒～

The Good Reads project is sponsored by
ABC Life Literacy Canada.

The project is funded in part by the Government of Canada's
Office of Literacy and Essential Skills.

Libraries and literacy and education markets
order from Grass Roots Press.

Bookstores and other retail outlets order from HarperCollins Canada.

Good Reads Series

If you enjoyed this Good Reads book,
you can find more at your local library or bookstore.

*

The Stalker by Gail Anderson-Dargatz

In From the Cold by Deborah Ellis

New Year's Eve by Marina Endicott

Home Invasion by Joy Fielding

The Day the Rebels Came to Town by Robert Hough

Missing by Frances Itani

Shipwreck by Maureen Jennings

The Picture of Nobody by Rabindranath Maharaj

The Hangman by Louise Penny

Easy Money by Gail Vaz-Oxlade

*

For more information on Good Reads,
visit **www.GoodReadsBooks.com**

Home Invasion
By Joy Fielding

Kathy Brown suddenly wakes up. Was that a noise in the house, or part of her dream?

In her dream, Kathy was about to kiss Michael, her high school boyfriend. Her husband, Jack, lies beside her, snoring. Michael is exciting. Jack is boring.

When Kathy hears the noise again, she gets up. Then she hears whispers. Then she feels a gun at her head. Two men are in the house. Kathy and her husband face a living nightmare. Kathy must also face her real feelings about her husband.

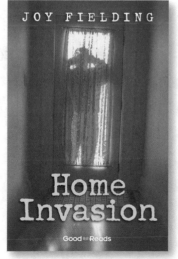

The outcome surprises everyone, most of all Kathy herself.

About the Author

 Anthony Hyde is best known for *The Red Fox*, the first of his spy novels. His father, Laurence Hyde, was an important artist. So, writing a story like *Picture This* came naturally to Anthony. Anthony was born in Ottawa, where he still lives.

Also by Anthony Hyde:

Promises, Promises
Double Helix
A Private House

SPY NOVELS:
The Red Fox
Formosa Straits
China Lake

*